I'm Glad God Thought of

MOTHERS

by Dot Cachiaras   Illustrated by Lorraine Arthur

ISBN: 0-87239-360-7

 STANDARD PUBLISHING
Cincinnati, Ohio   3630

One day I went out walking—
It's lots of fun to do—
I found some nice surprises,
Now, can *you* find them, too?

I noticed right away, when
I climbed up on the wall,
Our mother dog and puppy
Were playing with a ball!

Then out behind the rosebush,
  I thought I'd look for fun,
A mother cat and kitten
  Were sleeping in the sun!

Upon a rock was crawling
A busy ladybug;
I wondered if she had a
Baby bug to hug?

I ran down by the water,
   And this is what I found,
A mother duck and duckling
   Swimming 'round and 'round
   and 'round!

While squatting there I saw them,
So green upon a log,
Their legs stretched out for jump-
ing—
A mother and her baby frog!

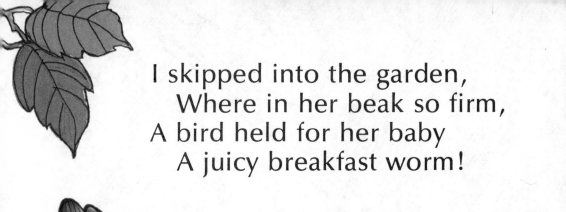

I skipped into the garden,
  Where in her beak so firm,
A bird held for her baby
  A juicy breakfast worm!

A mother rabbit hopped up
Between the lettuce rows,
And her little baby bunny
Was wiggling his pink nose!

Our mother cow was chewing
On purple clover sweet,
And swishing flies away from
Her calf down by her feet.

To quiet woods I hurried,
And there with head so low,
A darling spotted fawn was
Drinking with her doe.

I guess it wasn't naughty
For little pigs to do—
To wallow in the mud—since
Their mama was there, too!

The mother hen was calling
Her chickies, "Cluck-Cluck-
Clack!"
She seemed so very busy,
Just trying to keep track!

Our mare was in the pasture,
  And, with her big strong nose,
Her little colt she nuzzled—
  To show she cared, I s'pose!

A playful lamb so woolly
Ran back to take a leap,
Just trying to keep up with
His leaping mama sheep!

I ran back to our kitchen,
　　Where, on a baking spree,
Was my own love-y mother . . . and
　　Her little one was me!

I'm *glad* God thought of mothers
  Since creatures young and small
Need someone there to love them,
  And mothers do it best of all!